D0176301

CONTENTS

CHRONICLES OF NINJAGO™

AN OFFICIAL HANDBOOK

BY TRACEY WEST

Scholastic Inc.

ISBN 978-0-545-74638-0

LEGO, the LEGO logo, NINJAGO, the Brick and Knob configurations and the M...
Group. © 2015 The LEGO Group.
All rights reserved. Produced by Scholastic Inc. under license fr...
Published by Scholastic Inc. SCHOLASTIC and associated logos are tradema...
Scholastic Inc.

10 9 8 7 6 5 4 3 2 1   15 16 17 1...

Printed in the U.S.A.
First printing, January 2015

IT'S A WHOLE NEW WORLD

Kai, Cole, Jay, Zane, and Lloyd have been through a lot together. The five ninja faced off against a big evil: the Overlord. When the battle was over, the ninja won—but Ninjago™ City was left in ruins.

The people of Ninjago did what they always do—rebuild. They transformed their hometown into a fully automated city of the future: New Ninjago City.

But the ninja didn't know that the Overlord had survived as a computer virus. Cole, Jay, Kai, Lloyd, and Zane fought him again, as the Digital Overlord. This time, Zane made the ultimate sacrifice. He gave his life to save his friends—his family.

Is Zane truly gone? Cole, Jay, Kai, and Lloyd think so. But there is some hope. Pictures of Zane have been cropping up all over New Ninjago City. Could the Ninja of Ice have survived?

MASTER CHEN'S ISLAND

The ninja believe Zane might be on Master Chen's island. A massive red gate guards the entrance. Nobody can enter the island without Master Chen's permission.

Fortunately, the ninja have come as Master Chen's guests. Cole, Jay, Kai, and Lloyd received a mysterious message asking them to compete in a Tournament of Elements here on the island. The note contained a clue that Zane might be alive.

In this guide, you'll meet some of the new friends and foes the ninja will encounter on Master Chen's island. And you'll get an inside look at the next threat facing the Masters of Spinjitzu. Because there's no way of knowing what danger lurks around the corner . . .

THE NINJA

CHRONICLES

ACCESSING ZANE'S MEMORY BANKS...

Many things have happened since my friends Cole, Jay, Kai, and I were first trained in the art of Spinjitzu. Enemies have risen and fallen. Our home, Ninjago, has changed.

Keeping track of the chronicles of the ninja can be confusing. To assist my master, Sensei Wu, in his teaching, I have mined my database and compiled this time line of events. It begins in the past. As my master would say, "You must study the past before you can change the future."

THE FIRST SPINJITZU MASTER

Our story began when the First Master created the four Golden Weapons of Spinjitzu. He used their powers to create the island of Ninjago.

THE OVERLORD

The First Spinjitzu Master used the Golden Weapons to defeat a great evil known as the Overlord, who attacked Ninjago with his Stone Army. The First Spinjitzu Master cast the evil half of Ninjago, the Dark Island, into the sea.

TWO BROTHERS

The First Spinjitzu Master left the Weapons in the care of his two sons, Wu and Garmadon. As a boy, Garmadon was bitten by a snake known as the Great Devourer. The snake's venom slowly turned Garmadon evil. As teenagers, both brothers fell in love with a girl named Misako.

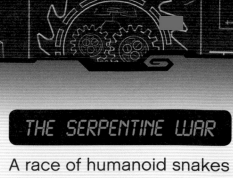

THE SERPENTINE WAR

A race of humanoid snakes called the Serpentine waged war on Ninjago. The snakes were defeated, and the Serpentine tribes were sealed off in tombs.

DIFFERENT BROTHERS, DIFFERENT PATHS

For many years, Wu studied Spinjitzu and became a teacher—a sensei. Garmadon married Misako. But then the evil venom completely took over him, transforming him into Lord Garmadon. He tried to take the Golden Weapons, but Wu cast him into the Underworld.

PROTECTING THE WEAPONS

Sensei Wu hid the Golden Weapons all across Ninjago. He left a map revealing their locations with someone he trusted: a blacksmith. Then Sensei Wu learned his brother was building a skeleton army to steal back the weapons. He sought out four young heroes to help him: myself, Jay, Cole, and the blacksmith's son, Kai.

Samukai, the leader of the skeleton army, kidnapped Kai's sister, Nya. Sensei Wu brought Kai to his monastery and trained him in the art of Spinjitzu. There he joined Cole, Jay, and me, and we learned that each of us had a different elemental power: Earth (Cole), Lightning (Jay), Fire (Kai), and Ice (me, Zane). Together we set out to rescue Nya and protect the weapons.

LORD GARMADON IS FREED

Lord Garmadon succeeded in taking the Weapons from us, but he could not hold them all himself. Instead, he tricked Samukai into holding them, creating a vortex that freed Garmadon from the Underworld. Samukai was destroyed, and we got hold of the weapons.

RISE OF THE SNAKES

Then we met Lloyd Garmadon, Lord Garmadon's son. As a young boy, Lloyd dreamed of being as powerful and evil as his father. He opened the Serpentine Tombs, releasing the imprisoned snakes. During our battles with the Serpentine, we were joined by a new ally—the mysterious Samurai X. We soon learned the samurai's true identity: Kai's sister, Nya!

LEGEND OF THE GREEN NINJA

We learned something else during this time: the legend of the Green Ninja. It told of a ninja strong enough to defeat the Overlord. Each of us wondered if we were the Green Ninja. But we had other things to worry about, too. We all wanted to find our true potential. We lost our home, the monastery, in a fire. I found a new home for us in an old ship called the *Destiny's Bounty*. Jay used his technical skills to make it fly.

SURPRISE AND BETRAYAL

Lloyd felt terrible about releasing the Serpentine. He joined our team and tried to stop them. He failed and was captured by Pythor, the last of the Anacondrai tribe. Pythor believed he was destined to reawaken the Great Devourer—the same snake whose venom had turned Garmadon evil.

FATHER AND SON

At this time, I discovered that I was not human, but a robot—a Nindroid. And we learned that Lord Garmadon had sprouted two extra arms so he could wield all four Golden Weapons at once. We rescued Lloyd—and found out he was the Green Ninja, destined to battle his own father. We had to let Garmadon use the Golden Weapons to battle the Great Devourer. Lord Garmadon was victorious, but he escaped with the Weapons.

THE MEGA WEAPON

Lord Garmadon trans-
formed the four Golden
Weapons into a Mega
Weapon capable of
creating—or destroying—
anything. During one of his attempts to destroy us,
Lloyd grew from a young boy into a young man. Then
Garmadon took the Mega Weapon back in time. We
followed him into the past and used the four original
Golden Weapons to destroy the Mega Weapon. The
Weapons merged and shot into space, where they
formed a new star.

THE DARK ISLAND

Cast out to sea, Lord
Garmadon encountered
the spirit of the Overlord
and raised the Dark
Island. Back in Ninjago,
the venom of the Great
Devourer brought the
Overlord's Stone Army
back to life. Working together, Lord Garmadon and the
Overlord tried to bring darkness to all of Ninjago. We
ninja traveled to the Dark Island, where we found the
Temple of Light. Inside, we gave up our elemental powers,
concentrating them on Lloyd so that he could become
the Golden Ninja.

THE ULTIMATE SPINJITZU MASTER

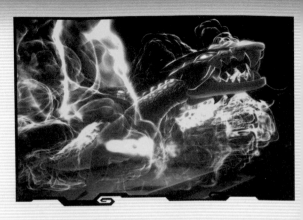

The prophecy said that Lloyd was the only one who could stop his father, but Garmadon did not want to fight his son. Then the Overlord took over Lord Garmadon's body, transforming into a huge, black dragon. Lloyd had no choice. He had to fight. During the battle, Lloyd became the Ultimate Spinjitzu Master. His power manifested itself in the Golden Dragon, which defeated the Overlord, freeing Garmadon and removing all the evil from him.

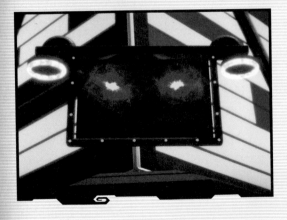

A NEW THREAT

The Overlord exploded in a blast of golden light, but his spirit did not die. When inventor Cyrus Borg rebuilt Ninjago City, the Overlord's spirit found a home in cyberspace. He forced Borg to copy Zane's blueprints and create an army of evil Nindroids. Then the Overlord took over all the technology in New Ninjago City. The Overlord needed one thing to return to the physical world—the power of the Golden Ninja.

LLOYD'S SACRIFICE

Pythor and the Digital Overlord managed to capture Lloyd and use his Golden Powers to bring the Overlord back into the real world. We ninja

entered the Digiverse to free him. Then Lloyd gave up his Golden Powers so the Overlord could not use them. Cole, Jay, Kai, and I regained our elemental powers. We learned we could use our elemental powers even without the Golden Weapons.

THE GOLDEN MASTER

The Overlord still had one last hope. He traveled to space to retrieve the four original Golden Weapons. He melted them down to create a suit of indestructible armor . . . and transformed himself into the Golden Master. Who could possibly defeat him?

In the battle against the Golden Master, I faced one of my greatest challenges yet. My friends thought I was lost forever. But if there is one thing I have learned about Ninjago, it is this: Good will always stand up to evil, and a ninja will never quit.

MEET THE HEROES AND VILLAINS

In Ninjago, life is always changing. And that means people are always changing, too.

After Lloyd defeated the Overlord, everyone had to get used to change. No longer evil, Lord Garmadon became the peaceful Sensei Garmadon. Without an enemy to defeat, Cole, Jay, Kai, and Zane became teachers at Sensei Wu's Academy.

And when the Overlord's spirit infected the computers of New Ninjago City, things changed again. Teachers became ninja. Good became evil, and evil became good. Some stories came to an end, while others were just beginning . . .

COLE

Cole is the Ninja of Earth. He's a strong, disciplined fighter who always tries to keep his feet on the ground, even when he's doing Spinjitzu.

Cole didn't set out to become a ninja. His father, Lou, wanted him to follow in his footsteps and become a performer in a barbershop quartet. When Cole couldn't cut it at the Marty Openheimer School of Performing Arts, he ran away. That's when he met Sensei Wu and began training to become a ninja.

In many ways, Cole is the rock of the ninja team—he's always focused, and he's always there when you need him. As the Ninja of Earth, he can make rocks to fly through the air and make the ground shake. That skill comes in handy when the ninja need to shake things up.

A NINJA DOESN'T SAVE HIMSELF—HE PROTECTS THOSE WHO CANNOT PROTECT THEMSELVES.

JAY

As the Ninja of Lightning, Jay has the speed and energy of a lightning bolt. He does everything quickly—moving, thinking, fighting, and especially joking.

Of all the ninja, Jay was the most excited about the technology in New Ninjago City. Cyrus Borg is a hero of his, and he was super-psyched to meet him. Jay is great at inventing things, a love that started in the junkyard he grew up in. He used to be embarrassed by his parents, Ed and Edna, and the junk they collected, but he's come to appreciate the devotion and ingenuity they've given him.

Always ready with a wisecrack, Jay is known as the funny ninja. No matter how serious a situation is, Jay is always ready with a joke. But though he might kid around while he fights, he takes his role as a ninja very seriously. He's creative in a fight, and he'll do whatever it takes to keep his friends—and all of Ninjago—safe from evil.

KAI

He's been called hotheaded, short-tempered, and careless. Kai definitely has a fiery personality, but that fire fuels his passion for justice. When there's a threat to Ninjago, Kai is the first one to jump into action.

Kai comes from humble beginnings—he once made his living as a blacksmith, like his father. All that changed when skeleton warriors kidnapped his sister, Nya. To save her, Kai learned to be a ninja.

He was the last ninja Sensei Wu recruited, and the last to achieve his full potential—when he saved Lloyd from the belly of an active volcano!

Kai has changed a lot since he first joined the ninja team. He was disappointed when he learned it wasn't his destiny to become the Green Ninja, but he quickly accepted his new mission—protecting and training Lloyd. That was the first step in mastering the fire within. Now he knows how to save that fire till it counts—in battle!

NINJA NEVER QUIT, AND NINJA WILL NEVER BE FORGOTTEN.

ZANE

When Zane first joined the ninja, he felt different, like an outsider. He had no memories of his past. Then he learned he was a robot, and that brought him some peace. He had a companion in his mechanical falcon. And he was finally reunited with his father, Dr. Julien, the man who created him. Even so, Zane felt there was nobody else like him in Ninjago, nobody who could understand.

Then Zane met Pixal, and everything changed. She was a Nindroid like him. They understood each other. He didn't feel alone anymore. When all of Ninjago lost power, Zane gave half of his unique power source to Pixal, forever connecting them.

He may be a Ninja of Ice, but Zane's mechanical heart is as warm as any human's. He sacrificed everything to defeat the Golden Master. His friends thought Zane was lost—but he rebuilt himself, becoming the Titanium Ninja.

I STAND FOR PEACE, FREEDOM, AND COURAGE IN THE FACE OF ALL WHO THREATEN NINJAGO.

LLOYD

Of all the ninja, Lloyd Garmadon has changed the most. When he was a young boy, he wanted to be just like his evil dad, Lord Garmadon. He opened the tombs containing the Serpentine, placing Ninjago in grave danger.

After the ninja captured him, Lloyd's uncle, Sensei Wu, showed him the error of his ways. When Lloyd uncovered his true potential, he found out he was the legendary Green Ninja. That meant he would have to battle his own father to save Ninjago.

Then the Overlord took over Lord Garmadon, and the final battle began. Lloyd transformed into the Golden Ninja—the Ultimate Spinjitzu Master—and defeated the Overlord.

But Lloyd's battle was not over. The Overlord returned, and he needed Lloyd's Golden Powers to make him stronger. To save Ninjago, Lloyd gave up his powers and became the Green Ninja once more.

Lloyd has grown into a strong, determined, and savvy ninja. But he is still young, with much to learn.

NYA

Like Sensei Wu, Nya was once briefly turned evil by the Overlord—but she got over it. That's a good thing, because Nya is the brains behind the ninja's operation.

When her brother, Kai, gets hotheaded, Nya keeps things steady. She comes up with a plan and sticks to it. And when the ninja are in over their heads, Nya sometimes shows up as her alter ego: Samurai X.

Nya is both a fierce fighter and a skilled inventor—she developed the Samurai X mech suit herself so she could make a difference in the battle against evil.

Cyrus Borg's technology caused some problems for Nya—but not in the way you might think. A "Perfect Match" machine analyzed her and told her she should be dating Cole instead of Jay. It wasn't evil technology, but it definitely gave Nya some headaches!

SENSEI WU

Sensei Wu—evil?! That's a difficult thing to imagine. This wise ninja has always fought to protect the innocent. He trained Cole, Jay, Kai, and Zane in the art of Spinjitzu, and he helped Lloyd transform from a bratty kid into a real hero.

Then the Overlord returned and threatened New Ninjago City. Sensei Wu allowed himself to be captured so the ninja could escape. The Overlord implanted evil technology into Sensei Wu, transforming him into Tech-Wu! He was completely under the Overlord's control.

When the ninja erased the Overlord from the Digiverse, Tech-Wu transformed back into Sensei Wu, and balance was restored to Ninjago— for a while.

SEARCH FOR THE POWER WITHIN, AND THEN REALIZE THE GREATNESS WITHIN EACH OTHER.

SENSEI GARMADON

Right now you might be wondering, how did evil Lord Garmadon become Sensei Garmadon? He can thank Lloyd for his transformation. The Overlord took over Lord Garmadon's body, and together they transformed into a huge, hideous black dragon. As the Golden Ninja, Lloyd destroyed the dragon and removed all the evil from his father.

Lord Garmadon became Sensei Garmadon. He reunited with his wife, Misako, and retreated to a monastery. He took a vow never to use weapons again, and taught his students how to "fight without fighting." But this vow of peace has proved difficult to uphold, between the Overlord's return and the appearance of Garmadon's old teacher, Master Chen . . .

> KNOW THY ENEMY, BUT MORE IMPORTANT, KNOW THY FRIEND.

MISAKO

Misako is an archaeologist at the Ninjago Museum of History. Her wisdom and knowledge of history has helped the ninja defeat enemies who rise from the past, like the Stone Army. She's also proved her bravery, allowing herself to be captured by the Stone Army in order to protect Lloyd and the ninja.

Misako is Lloyd's mother and Sensei Garmadon's wife. When she was younger, she had feelings for both Wu and Garmadon. For years, she wasn't sure if she made the right choice. But now that Garmadon is no longer evil, Misako seems at peace with her decision.

I MIGHT NOT BE A NINJA, BUT I CAN LOOK AFTER MYSELF!

DARETH

When the ninja first stepped into Dareth's Grand Sensei Mojo Dojo Academy, they thought he was, well, a loser. He bragged about ninja powers he didn't have. But since then, Dareth has proved himself to be a valuable member of the team.

Dareth accidentally put on Lord Garmadon's helmet, which allowed him to control the Overlord's Stone Army. He has the awesome ability to speak to sharks, and he used it to save the students of Sensei Wu's Academy. And he has amazing hair. Those are just some of the reasons he's earned the title the "Brown Ninja."

THAT'S MR. BROWN NINJA TO YOU, SALLY!

THE SERPENTINE

Long before time had a name, the humans of Ninjago waged war against five ancient snake tribes. When the humans won, the snakes were banished to Ninjago's underground and sealed into tombs. There they lived for many years, until the day Lloyd Garmadon opened the tombs and set the snakes free.

The five tribes are:

THE ANACONDRAI

The Anacondrai are the most powerful and fearsome of all the snakes. Humans have long been fascinated by this Serpentine tribe, and it's even believed some people worshiped its members. The Anacondrai's chameleon-like scales allow them to disguise themselves and effectively disappear. Today, the only surviving member of the tribe is Pythor.

THE CONSTRICTAI

The strongest of the Serpentine, these snakes' constricting bodies can crush solid stone. Once they get a hold of something, they'll never let it go. The Constrictai can also quickly burrow through the ground for surprise attacks on their prey.

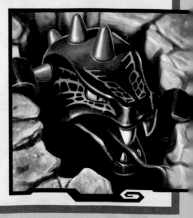

THE FANGPYRES

Much like a vampire's, a Fangpyre's bite can transform any living or non-living thing into one of their own. The Fangpyre's favorite attack strategy is the jump attack, which allows them to flatten their bodies and glide through the air.

THE HYPNOBRAI

These powerful snake charmers can use their hypnotic eyes to control others' minds, as Cole learned the hard way!

THE VENOMARI

The Venomari's strongest weapon is their venom. The acid they spit eats through the thickest of armor, causing its victims to hallucinate their deepest and darkest fears.

THE GREAT DEVOURER

According to ancient legend, The Great Devourer is a snake that grows the more it consumes. After Pythor reawakened the enormous snake, it took all the combined power of the ninja, Lord Garmadon, and Lloyd to defeat it.

SCALES

A snake transforms when it sheds its skin. Scales, leader of the Hypnobrai, transformed from one of the ninja's deadliest enemies to an unlikely ally.

SSSORRY, YOU'VE GOT THE WRONG SSSNAKE!

After Lloyd released the Serpentine from their underground prison, Scales rose in the ranks to rule the entire Serpentine tribe. It was his idea to have the tribes dig under Ninjago City so he could doom the people of Ninjago to their own underground prison.

Later, when the ninja learned that a mysterious Serpentine was helping the Digital Overlord, they suspected Scales. But they discovered that he had settled down to a peaceful life with his wife, Selma, and his son, Scales, Jr.

Scales welcomed the ninja to the Serpentine world and told them the Legend of the Golden Master. From that moment on, they could count on a truce with Scales and the Serpentine tribes.

PYTHOR

THISSS ISSSN'T OVER!

Pythor is the last surviving member of the Anacondrai tribe. When the ninja battled the Serpentine, he led the charge to revive the Great Devourer and claim Ninjago for the snakes. Pythor succeeded in bringing the reptile back to life—only to be consumed by the Devourer. It looked like he was gone forever.

But Pythor reappeared in New Ninjago City, wearing a hooded cloak to conceal his identity. He helped the Digital Overlord capture Lloyd and steal his Golden Power.

These days, Pythor has two new looks. Trapped inside the Great Devourer's gut, he was bleached white from stomach acid. And when he intercepted a nano pill meant for the Overlord, he was shrunk down to fun size. Is this the last the ninja will see of him? Only time will tell …

THE DIGITAL OVERLORD

> ONCE I RID THE SCOURGE THAT IS THE NINJA, I WILL WALK NINJAGO WITH THE POWER TO RULE THIS WORLD AND BEYOND!

As ancient as Ninjago itself, the Overlord might be evil in its purest form. He created the Stone Army and fought the First Spinjitzu Master. But the master prevailed, and banished the Overlord to the Dark Island.

Many years later, Lloyd faced the Overlord. The Overlord swallowed him whole, but the Golden Power inside him exploded, healing Ninjago.

Somehow, the Overlord's spirit survived and went into hiding in cyberspace. His goal was to steal Lloyd's Golden Power and use it to return to physical form.

So Lloyd gave up his Golden Power. The Overlord sent Nindroids into space to retrieve the original Golden Weapons. He used them to become the terrifying Golden Master. It looked like all hope was lost, but Zane sacrificed himself to destroy the Golden Master and save Ninjago.

CYRUS BORG

Lloyd's first battle with the Overlord made a mess out of Ninjago City. Inventor Cyrus Borg stepped in to rebuild, and New Ninjago City was born.

Borg believed in the power of technology to improve life. But he made one big mistake: He built the headquarters of Borg Industries over the ashes of the Overlord. The Digital Overlord took over Borg. As the OverBorg, the Digital Overlord could move around in the physical world again.

When the ninja shut down the power in Ninjago City, the Digital Overlord lost his hold on Borg—but not for long. The Nindroids captured him, and the Digital Overlord transformed him into the half-human, half-droid Evil Borg. Only the destruction of the Digital Overlord returned him to his original form.

> I'VE INVENTED SIX MECHANICAL LEGS SO I CAN CLIMB UP WALLS. THERE'S NOTHING MY MIND CAN'T FIX.

PIXAL

Pixal was created by Cyrus Borg as his assistant. Her name stands for "Primary Interactive Xternal Assistant Lifeform." She remained loyal to her creator until the Digital Overlord infected her with evil and sent her to take the Techno-Blades from the ninja.

Zane intercepted Pixal and used his Techno-Blade to get rid of the program corrupting her. Pixal returned the favor by alerting the ninja to a Nindroid attack. She became one of the ninja's most valuable allies—and a good friend to Zane.

When the ninja cut off the power to New Ninjago City, Pixal's power source died, too. Zane healed her by giving her half of his own unique power source, forever linking them. While Zane became weaker, Pixal found her fighting skills had improved. She proved she would do whatever she could to protect the ninja and save Ninjago.

> ZANE SAVED MY LIFE. WHEN I WAS WITH HIM, I FELT A CONNECTION. I FELT . . . FREE.

THE NINDROIDS

The Digital Overlord used Cyrus Borg to create this army of robot ninja. They are based on Zane's blueprints, but they are faster, stronger, and bounce back more quickly than any of the Masters of Spinjitzu.

When the ninja take to the sky, the Nindroids sprout wings and fly, propelled by jets in their feet. They are also equipped with cloaking devices so they can hide in plain sight. And Lloyd's Golden Powers can't stop them—in fact, his powers only make them stronger!

MASTER CHEN

Master Chen has two faces: One is the beloved owner of a chain of popular noodle shops in Ninjago; the other is a crime lord who runs the Tournament of Elements.

Rolling in noodle money, Chen lives in a palace on his own private island. He has a past with Sensei Garmadon, who doesn't trust him. When the Serpentine first battled Ninjago, Chen turned against his own kind and sided with the treacherous snakes. Now there are symbols of the Anacondrai tribe all over his temple. There are still lots of worshippers of the Anacondrai ... Could Chen be one of them? To Garmadon, it's very suspicious.

Sensei Garmadon knows the Tournament of Elements is more than just a fighting contest—but what exactly is Master Chen up to?

CLOUSE

Master Chen's right-hand man looks like a distinguished butler. He is also a spell caster who will use magic or whatever else it takes to stop the ninja from winning the tournament.

Like his master, Clouse has a history with Garmadon. Based on the way they speak to each other, it's not a good one.

THE ELEMENTAL WARRIORS

F ighters from all over Ninjago have been invited to the Tournament of Elements. Each one is descended from an Elemental Master. Some possess powers the ninja have never seen before.

KARLOF

This bulky brute can harness the power of metal to turn himself into a walking, talking piece of steel. He's brawny, but he doesn't seem to be much in the brains department.

SKYLOR

Skylor is a determined competitor in the Tournament of Elements. But when Kai asks her what her elemental power is, she replies, "Wouldn't you like to know?"

Kai is instantly attracted to Skylor. And this mysterious beauty is not afraid to use his feelings to further her own goals in the competition.

GRAVIS

A Master of Gravity, Gravis can walk on walls and ceilings. He can also use the power of gravity to move objects in space—a handy skill in combat.

TURNER

T urner is a Master of Speed. "Master of Speed? That's not an element," Jay observed when he first met Turner.

"So says the Master of Lightning," Sensei Garmadon pointed out.

BOLOBO

T his ninja can harness the power of nature, ensnaring his opponents in twisted vines that spring from nowhere.

NEURO

Neuro is Master of Mind. He can read his opponents' minds and predict their next moves. He also knows how to give the enemy one heck of a headache.

ASH

Ash is Master of Smoke. He can explode into a cloud of smoke, then swirl and reform himself. It's hard to land a blow against Ash because he can transform himself at any moment.

NEW ENEMIES, NEW WEAPONS

When the ninja first learned Spinjitzu, they used dragons to get where they needed to go. Their Golden Weapons possessed ancient powers.

In New Ninjago City, old school was out, and technology ruled. There the ninja wielded the Techno-Blades in order to fight the Digital Overlord.

Now the ninja are on Master Chen's mysterious island—an island that does not appear on any known maps. Here they will depend solely on their elemental powers . . .

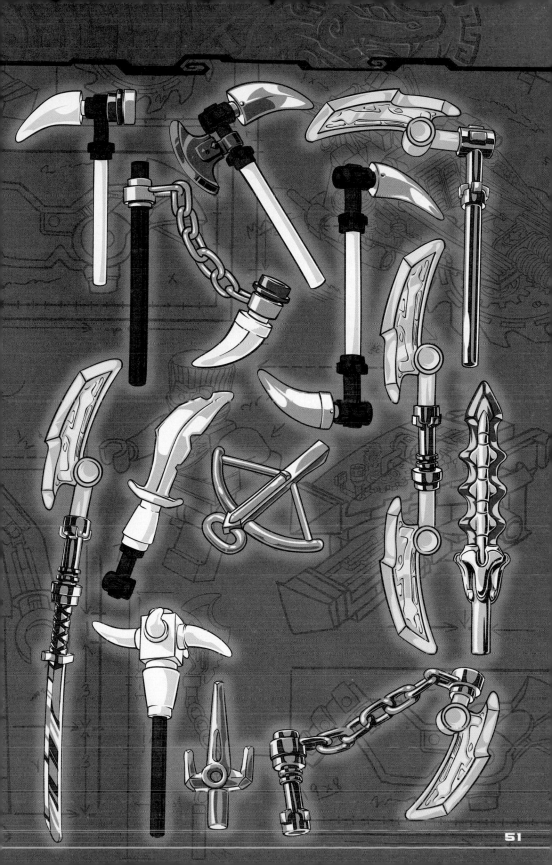

THE GOLDEN WEAPONS
(THE FOUR WEAPONS OF SPINJITZU)

The Golden Weapons are powerful arms created by the First Spinjitzu Master, who harnessed their power to create the land of Ninjago. The Weapons' guardians were Wu and Garmadon, the sons of the First Spinjitzu Master.

When Garmadon turned to the dark side, Wu hid the Golden Weapons to keep them safe. When Ninjago was under threat, Wu recruited Cole, Jay, Kai, and Zane and made each the protector of one of the weapons. Each weapon is tied to its ninja's elemental powers.

Cole was master of the Scythe of Quakes, which could make the ground tremble and crack. It was the first Golden Weapon. The First Spinjitzu Master used it to help form the mountains, hills, and valleys of Ninjago.

Zane was guardian of the Shurikens of Ice. Anything the shurikens struck froze instantly. Their power was used to create the frozen northern and southern regions of Ninjago.

Kai's Golden Weapon was the Dragon Sword of Fire. Believed to be the most powerful of the four Weapons, anything the sword struck instantly burst into flames. According to legend, the Fire Dragon's power may have helped create the Sword of Fire.

The Nunchuks of Lightning unleashed sizzling bolts of lightning powerful enough to shatter stone. Because of their electric nature, they were dangerous to touch—for everyone but Jay, Ninja of Lightning.

Garmadon eventually got his hands on the Golden Weapons and forged them into one all-powerful Mega Weapon, which could create or destroy anything. The ninja managed to wrest the Mega Weapon from Garmadon, sending it into space. Eventually, the Golden Weapons were claimed by the Nindroids for the Overlord, who had them melted down into armor so he could become the Golden Master.

THE TECHNO-BLADES

Cyrus Borg invented the Techno-Blades to stop the Digital Overlord. He gave them to Kai with the warning, "Please protect them with your life! All of Ninjago depends on it!"

A few minutes later, Nindroids attacked the ninja. Cole, Jay, Kai, and Zane didn't have much time to figure out how to use their new weapons. The blades' dull edges couldn't cut through the metal of enemy vehicles. So what were they good for?

Zane figured it out first—the Techno-Blades don't behave like other weapons. They can hack into machinery and transform ordinary objects into highly advanced vehicles. When activated, each ninja's elemental power runs through the blade, revealing the machine's circuitry and transforming it into a supercharged ninja vehicle.

Zane's blade turns icy blue when it activates. He used it to create his NinjaCopter.

Kai's blade turns red. He used it to create his Kai Fighter.

Jay's blade turns electric yellow. He used it to create his Thunder Raider.

Cole's green blade is attached to the end of a long chain. He used it to create his Earth Mech.

The ninja also wielded their Techno-Blades in the Digiverse during their epic battle against the Digital Overlord. Working together, they used the blades to reboot the system and permanently erase the Overlord.

LOCATIONS

In the early days, Cole, Jay, Kai, and Zane learned Spinjitzu in Sensei Wu's monastery. There they learned to trust one another and work as a team. When the monastery burned down, they roamed Ninjago, looking for a new home. Along the way, they learned something important: Home could be anywhere, as long as they were together.

Since then, the ninja have traveled all over Ninjago, and even into space! Here are just a few of the places the ninja have explored.

SENSEI WU'S ACADEMY

This tall, pagoda-like building sits on the outskirts of New Ninjago City. It used to be Darkley's Boarding School for Bad Boys, where Lloyd was sent when he was young.

After Lloyd first defeated the Overlord and the Serpentine were safely back underground, the ninja had no more enemies to fight. Sensei Wu transformed the school into Sensei Wu's Academy, and Cole, Jay, Kai, Zane, and Nya became teachers there. Until the Digital Overlord threatened Ninjago once more . . .

DESTINY'S BOUNTY

Zane discovered this deserted ship soon after the Serpentine raided and destroyed Sensei Wu's monastery. The ninja quickly transformed the *Destiny's Bounty* into a cozy new home. And then Jay programmed the ship to fly!

The ninja later learned that the *Destiny's Bounty* had a long and interesting history. It was once a pirate ship helmed by the fearsome Captain Soto. When Lord Garmadon accidentally used the Mega-Weapon to bring Captain Soto and his crew back to life, the ninja had to fight the pirates. They won—but Lord Garmadon escaped with the *Bounty* before Cole, Jay, Kai, and Zane could stop him!

SENSEI GARMADON'S MONASTERY

After the evil left Lord Garmadon, he gave up violence and retreated to this sanctuary in the countryside. It is a peaceful place surrounded by green orchards. Inside, Garmadon—now Sensei Garmadon—trains pupils in the Art of the Silent Fist: to fight without fighting.

Cole, Jay, Kai, Zane, and Lloyd came to the monastery for a visit and briefly trained with Sensei Garmadon. That training came in handy soon afterward, when Nindroids attacked the monastery. To keep them from getting their hands on Lloyd's Golden Power, Garmadon and Lloyd had to flee. Time will tell if they will ever return . . .

NEW NINJAGO CITY

The Overlord's attack decimated Ninjago City. In the aftermath, the citizens came together, working hard to rebuild. Cyrus Borg led them, and invented technology to make the city better and brighter. New Ninjago City was born.

Skyscrapers rose from the dust. Hover cars whizzed through the air. Buses were replaced by a sleek monorail. Automated machines filled everyone's needs, and robot workers served the public. Above it all loomed Borg Tower, the headquarters of Borg Industries.

All this technology needed a lot of power, so Borg built a huge, hovering power station outside the city. The station captured energy from electrically charged winds.

SAMURAI X'S SECRET LAIR

Nya sure is busy. Somehow, between helping the ninja as Samurai X and teaching at Sensei Wu's Academy, she found the time to build a secret underground lab. Nobody—not even Sensei Wu—knew about it.

That made it the perfect hiding place for Lloyd. The entrance to the lair is in the desert, through the skull of an enormous dinosaur skeleton. Inside, Nya develops prototypes for new samurai vehicles, including the speedy Samurai Raider.

MASTER CHEN'S ISLAND

The setting for the Tournament of Elements is a mysterious private island that belongs to Master Chen. No one knows how to reach the island, and guests can only enter with permission from Master Chen.

A large, walled-in palace rises from the island's center. The ninja will soon discover there's more to this palace than meets the eye—underneath it is a warren of hidden chambers and tunnels.

Where do all these tunnels and rooms lead? And why does a rich man like Master Chen need to make his home so far from the Ninjago mainland? Cole, Jay, Kai, and Lloyd must answer these questions if they hope to find Zane . . .

WHAT'S NEXT FOR THE NINJA?

After Zane sacrificed himself to take down the Golden Master and save Ninjago, his friends thought he was gone forever. They didn't know that Zane had rebuilt himself into a stronger, better Zane—the Titanium Ninja.

Then Cole, Jay, Kai, and Lloyd learned that Zane might be alive, and on Master Chen's Island. To get to the island, the ninja had to agree to participate in a Tournament of Elements.

When Sensei Garmadon discovered what the ninja were up to, he joined them. He knew they were up against a force much greater than they realized.

How does the tournament work? Master Chen has created a series of challenges. A fighter will be eliminated in each—until only one remains standing.

What happens to the losers? That's a question Cole, Jay, Kai, and Lloyd want to answer. And what will the winner receive? The ninja don't know that, either, but it's not important for now. Their goal is to save Zane, and they know he's on the island somewhere.

But what is Master Chen up to? The ninja soon realize that Garmadon is right to be suspicious. Now they must fight to find Zane . . . and stop Master Chen.

As long as there is something worth fighting for, there will always be a need for a ninja . . . and Cole, Jay, Kai, Lloyd, Nya, and their friends will always be there!